THE BEST OF
BEETLE BAILEY

THE BEST OF BEETLE BAILEY

BY MORT WALKER
A Thirty-three Year Treasury

DESIGNED AND EDITED BY
BRIAN WALKER

AN AUTHORS GUILD BACKINPRINT.COM EDITION

AN AUTHORS GUILD BACKINPRINT.COM EDITION
Published by iUniverse, Inc.

For information address:
iUniverse, Inc.
2021 Pine Lake Road, Suite 100
Lincoln, NE 68512
www.iuniverse.com

Originally published by Comicana

**All Beetle Bailey comic strips copyright © 1950, 1951, 1952, 1953, 1954, 1955, 1956,
1957, 1958, 1959, 1960, 1961, 1962, 1963, 1964, 1965, 1966, 1967, 1968, 1969, 1970,
1971, 1972, 1973, 1974, 1975, 1976, 1977, 1978, 1979, 1980, 1981, 1982, 1983 and 1984
by King Features Syndicate, Inc.
All other artwork copyright © by Mort Walker**

Library of Congress Catalog Card Number: 83-63535

**Cover Design by Robert Reed
Layout assistance by Abby Gross and Neal Walker
Typography by Tod Clonan Associates, Inc.**

**The cartoons in this book have appeared in newspapers
in the United States and abroad under the auspices of
King Features Syndicate, Inc.**

Special thanks to the Museum of Cartoon Art

ISBN-13: 978-0-595-34848-0
ISBN-10: 0-595-34848-3

Printed in the United States of America

"Success isn't funny; failure is."

HAGAR
The Horrible

DIK BROWNE

1950 was a helluva year to start a comic strip.

A famous editor had just decided that the comics were the "sick chicks" of the daily newspapers . . . an even more famous cartoonist had stated that within 10 years only four strips would still be appearing . . . the Korean War had started and TV had just exploded on the national consciousness.

As it turned out 1950 was a vintage year for the comic strip.

Two of the greatest comic strips of all times started that year — "Peanuts" and "Beetle Bailey".

Both began modestly — Beetle with only 12 papers and there was some fear that it might not survive. Did it ever! Beetle survived the Korean War . . . censorship by the Brass . . . an unpopular war in Vietnam . . . a rising tide of hostility toward all things military . . . to emerge, at last, 30 years later — still a goof-off, an unpromoted private and the most famous soldier since Napolean was a corporal, read by over 150,000,000 people in more than 1500 papers.

Now there are thousands of strips submitted every year. Hundreds of these must have been Army strips. What could account for Beetle's unique success?

The answer, of course, is the unequaled comic genius of its creator (my friend) MORT WALKER.

Among the many awards his fellow-cartoonists have given him, one (the Elzie Segar award) is given for the artist who is best able to create his own comic strip world . . . No cartoonists ever filled these specifications better than Mort. Camp Swampy isn't merely an Army Camp. It is a microcosm of the world peopled by delightful lunatics, each endowed with an unforgettable character by its creator.

It's hard to write about Mort without using the word creator a lot.

Mort is almost compulsively creative, a condition that since the advent of Beetle has led to six additional comic strips, countless books, countless children and countless projects, including the founding of the Museum of Cartoon Art.

Mort is truly the Cartoonists' Cartoonist.

Which is odd, because no one looks less like a cartoonist than Mort.

Soft of speech, abnormally normal in appearance (he is the bane of caricaturists); his clothes don't even look funny.

Cartoonists are supposed to model their characters after themselves — here again Mort defies the form chart.

Beetle Bailey's "schtick" is, of course, his unending struggle to avoid labor in any form. Mort is equally passionate in his search for new work to be done.

Together they have given us a classic comic strip. The answer to their success may be "Speak softly and carry a BIG schtick . . ."

And now to introduce the man who really needs no introduction, I give you Beetle Bailey . . .

Sarasota, Florida
1982

THE FIRST STEP

Introduction
by Mort Walker

1950

A journey of a thousand miles begins with the first step, they say, but watch out for that first step, it's a biggie. Starting a comic strip is like stepping out into darkness. Who knows where it will lead you? I didn't.

Few people remember that Beetle Bailey began as a comic strip about college life. Beetle also had eyes (closed). Few people remember because the strip appeared in so few papers.

As a practical matter of survival the strip was soon changed to a military theme. All the original characters (except Beetle) were discarded and new ones created. That is what's fun about doing a comic strip, you're not stuck with your first mistake, you're free to make new mistakes at any time. For instance, Sarge originally had a wife and kids. When that theme became cumbersome, I conveniently forgot his family and left them out there in limbo somewhere.

1951

1952

I've always subscribed to the philosophy, "When something doesn't work, try something else." Going down with the ship is for dead heroes. Over the years new characters have been introduced, found boring and been given the gate. Sarge's tooth traveled all around his mouth till it found a home in the rear of his lower jaw.

Then

Sarge's shape changed from slim to fat and Beetle shrunk from a lanky string bean to normal size and weight. Camp Swampy went through several attempts to give it more character and ended up an amorphous mess forgotten and ignored by the Pentagon. Nobody can criticize Camp Swampy for being inaccurate when it comes to modern military procedures because it's in a world all its own disowned by the army, civilian life and time itself.

1960

1970

The strip has been through many turmoils, banned by the army, censored by editors, attacked by special interest groups but it's a survivor. Someone said a diamond is just a piece of coal that stuck with the job. To me the strip is a diamond. I never knew where that first step would take me and there were many rocky times, but a certain amount of fame and fortune were my reward for keeping at it.

I've enjoyed every moment of the trip, though. So many wonderful people I've met along the way, some important, but mostly just good people who like to laugh. And it's been my joy to think that I've added to the good humor of the past thirty-so years.

Hope you enjoy the book.

1980

Now

Mort Walker, portrait by Stan Drake

MATRICULATION

The Strip Is Born

Contrary to King Features announcement on the launching of the strip, there weren't many big cheers for Beetle in the beginning. It started September 4, 1950, in only 12 papers and moved very slowly. After six months it had signed on only 25 clients. Strips are not considered to be on solid ground unless they are sold to at least 100 papers.

King Features Syndicate publicity, 1950

We decided not to run this strip and never show Beetle's eyes to help identify him. He sleeps with his hat on, takes showers, and everyone accepts it.

The first strip

No-one knew why the college theme didn't go over. Maybe it wasn't typical of the experiences of most readers. Anyway, King Features (unbeknownst to me) was considering dropping it after a year's contract was up. In the meantime I was blithely scratching away, loving my work and happy to be making the royal sum of $150 a week that King was paying me.

These first strips have never been republished or seen by more than a handful of readers so we thought a selection of them would be of interest.

Beetle's character began to emerge. He subscribes to the philosophy, "Whenever the urge to work comes over me, I lie down until it goes away." But in his classes he always manages to scrape through by the skin of someone else's teeth.

When it comes to romance, Beetle is about as smooth as a porcupine with skin problems. He probably would have been more thoughtful, considerate and attentive, but those words weren't in his male chauvinist's handbook.

My fraternity house was a menagerie of characters, a living comic strip. There was the rich man's kid, "Diamond Jim," the scholar, "Plato," the campus jock, "Sweatsock," the guy who couldn't be pleased, "Bitter Bill," and an eccentric teacher, "Prof. Jesse Wrench." Those were just a few of the friends I put into cartoon form.

College Days Are Over

When the Korean War heated up, college boys began being drafted right and left. Since I had painted Beetle as the campus clown, he was destined to get his hiking papers. Rather than wait for the draft I thought he should bumble right into uniform. Fate was kind. The army theme was just what a failing strip needed. It quickly added 100 papers and has never stopped growing since. In spite of this my King Features editor said, "If you'd brought us an army strip in the first place, we never would have bought it."

King Features Syndicate publicity, 1951

Pvt. Beetle

Beetle was assimilated into army life rapidly. Instead of dorm mates he simply switched to barracks buddies. Instead of professors who gave him trouble, he had sergeants. Instead of institutional food in the cafeteria he got his heartburn in the mess hall. He fell right into it . . . especially the bed.

First Sketches Showing Beetle In Uniform When He Entered Army 1951

Sarge (Orville P. Snorkel)

When Beetle joined the army he need someone to keep him in line. Sarge was the result.

Sarge is probably my favorite character to draw. Not only does he look funny in all positions, but he takes up a lot of space which saves me from drawing a lot of backgrounds. He's garrulous, profane, ecstatic, rough, sentimental, voracious . . . he does everything to the extreme. At first his only characteristic was meanness. He was much leaner and I couldn't decide how many fangs a proper sergeant should have. But he gradually took shape like a blimp in full bloom. He beats up on his boys at one moment and takes them out for a beer at the next, and it all seems natural.

CANTEEN, who was always eating   **SNAKE EYES, the barracks gambler**

Early Characters Who Didn't Make It.

In the creation of a strip you're not sure what the public will like. So you try something and, if it doesn't work, you try something else. I'm always experimenting in layout, gag styles and art techniques. But mostly, I experiment with new characters. Here's a sampling that made a bow and got the hook.

BIG BLUSH, tall, innocent and a great attraction to the girls

FIREBALL, the neophyte who always seems to be in the way.

BAMMY, the southern patriot who is still fighting the civil war.

DAWG, the guy in every barracks who creates his own pollution.

GENERAL HALFTRACK is what every GI knows a general is . . . he's lousy at running the camp and when he gets home his wife runs him.

Cookie as he first appeared in 1952

Early Versions of Characters Who Settled In.

It takes awhile for a character to jell. Like a new friend you need to get to know him. His shape has to be worked out till you can recognize him from all angles, even in silhouette. You have to decide what he can and can't do to keep him consistent. He slowly grows before your eyes until one day, BINGO!

Here are some early versions of characters who are still around today.

ZERO is the naive farm boy with the innocent heart of a child. At one time I decided his buck teeth made him too much like the sterotype dumb guy found throughout comic strip history so I dropped him. After several months I ran into Ernie Bushmiller (creator of "Nancy") who said he missed him. Back came Zero.

KILLER was patterned after an army roomate who thought he was God's gift to women. He wasn't especially gift wrapped attractively but he had a direct approach which got him what he wanted about every 50th try.

COOKIE is a summation of so many army chefs I was victimized by. They were a bunch of slobs, usually whose main talent was making you lose your appetite. I later gave him a chef's hat to help his identity.

CAPT. SCABBARD was inspired by a Capt. Johnson I once served under. On a hike he used to carry a canteen filled with gin. We were always getting lost.

The best ideas come from personal experience, as in the above strip. The bulletin said there were ten openings for Officer's School and I asked permission to take the test. My sergeant thought it humorous that a mere private should have such lofty ambitions. When his laughter subsided he gave me permission. Four hundred applicants showed up for the test. I took one look and recognized it as a test I'd taken before. I breezed through it and was on the train for OCS that night.

When Beetle first started it only appeared during the week.
The Sunday page started 2 years later.

The First Sunday Page — September 14, 1952

The only appearance of Sarge's wife.

THE LONG MARCH

G.I. Bailey

Beetle represents the typical downtrodden G.I. Joe (The G.I. stands for "Government Issued," which is the degree of anonymity most G.I.s feel). They're herded like cattle, treated like dirt and praised for being the protectors of our freedom . . . which they give up the minute they join the army. Their duty, as they see it is to work as hard as possible to avoid work . . . then stay up all night having fun.

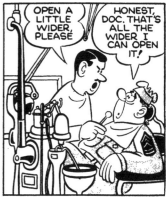

Top Sergeant Snorkel

Top sergeants have been called the backbone of the army. Most GI's refer to them as a lower part of the anatomy. They make a fetish out of being tough but are often rather childlike offstage. Most of them are career army types who are so immersed in military life they think a civilian is a soldier in drag.

Sgt. Snorkel is the epitome of that breed.

AND HOW ABOUT A CITATION FOR ALL THOSE DANGEROUS MISSIONS TO TOWN IN THAT BROKEN-DOWN CAMP BUS?!

I HOLD THE RECORD FOR FLIES SWATTED IN THE MESS HALL! THAT SHOULD BE WORTH **SOMETHING**!

THE BIVOUAC RIBBON: BLUE FOR RAIN, BROWN FOR MUD, WINTERGREEN FOR MOSQUITOES, WITH A POISON IVY WREATH.

AND WE OUGHTA HAVE A UNIT EMBLEM TOO!

9-12

Zero

We all know someone like Zero who isn't quite with it. His name is a clue to his I.Q. But he's not really as mentally deficient as he is uninformed. I get letters occasionally saying that I'm making fun of retarded people. Of course I'm not. Zero couldn't be in the army if he were retarded. He's just an innocent young farm boy as sweet, honest and unsophisticated as an ear of corn. You couldn't find a better friend, he makes you feel so superior.

Killer Diller

Every barracks has a guy like Killer who spends every waking hour thinking of girls and every sleeping hour next to one (hopefully). One of the famous cartoon series during World War II was "The Wolf." He had a normal human body with the head of a wolf, and his ears wiggled in proximity to any female. I adapted the idea and used Killer's barracks cap peaks as the ears.

2-27

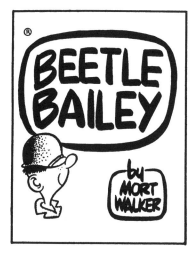

2-20

General Amos T. Halftrack

As a leader, General Halftrack couldn't lead a cub scout to a candy store, but he's one of my favorite characters to work with. In the beginning I put a lot of my own feelings and experiences into the Beetle character. As time wore on I discovered I was relating more to the General and I'm coming up with a lot more gags on him as a result. I guess he's just a grown-up goof-up like me.

LT. SONNY FUZZ. It is a humorous situation to have a young, eager, newly-minted lieutenant arrive and start bossing around the old grizzled incumbent first sergeant. I was 21 when I did it and I know now who won . . . the sergeant!

CHAPLAIN STANEGLASS. It's also funny to see someone try to be a moral influence on a bunch of rambunctious young bucks who are away from home, horny and thirsty. Staneglass tries, but as the Chaplain's magazine mourned, "He is ineffectual."

ROCKY. At first he played the role as a young hood from a street gang but, as times changed, he became more anti-establishment, running the underground newspaper and agitating for any current cause.

The day after this strip . . .

Beetle Is Banned From The Stars and Stripes

Probably the best favor the Army did for me since discharging me was banning me from the STARS AND STRIPES. It became a tempest in a teapot and the ensuing publicity rocketed Beetle's circulation another hundred papers overnight.

After the Korean War was over the brass felt they needed to tighten up discipline. In combat, staying clean is not as important as staying alive. But when the fighting is over the polishing returns. Naturally there was some resistance to spit-and-polish by battle hardened veterans. The brass felt Beetle Bailey wasn't helping their program. Beetle was making fun of authority and romanticizing foot-dragging. From this myopic point of view, Beetle had to go.

It was a mistake on their part. It only revealed what everyone knew all along. The military big wigs don't have a sense of humor. A sense of humor is a sign of maturity and a person with intelligence and confidence can laugh at himself. At least that's what all the news stories and broadcasts said. It made the brass look petty and ridiculous.

I thank them again for their steady supply of funny material.

Journal NEW YORK American

TRUTH, JUSTICE   PUBLIC SERVICE

THURSDAY, JANUARY 14, 1954   ★

Beetle Bailey Ban

MOMENTOUS military decisions of the past week give indication to thinkers that the Pentagon is not expecting another war.

The first is an order that Navy officers must wear swords again.

The second is a ban on "Beetle Bailey" in the Tokyo edition of Stars and Stripes, the GI newspaper.

Both orders are designed to increase, or at least protect, the prestige of officers.

Return of the swords starts with the top brass and goes thence down the line, presumably in direct proportion to the need for enhanced dignity.

For the benefit of the few, if any, who didn't know, "Beetle Bailey" is Mort Walker's delightful comic strip, carried in the Journal-American, which gently kids an "eagle colonel" as freely as a yardbird. Apparently Beetle has offended someone's dignity.

The reason that we think these orders are harbingers of peace is that if an appreciable number of reservists were called back to active duty, on threat of war, they would laugh both rulings right out of existence.

Newspaper articles about the STARS AND STRIPES ban, 1954

Making the Most of the Ban

The STARS AND STRIPES ban lasted over ten years but it didn't keep the G.I.'s from seeing Beetle Bailey. We kept hitting away with publicity and encouraged readers to clip and send the strip to their soldiers. It worked and it put my circulation on an uphill course that never stopped. I think it also made me hit away harder at the ineptness and inconsistencies I found in the military process.

Send your soldier in the far east something he wants...

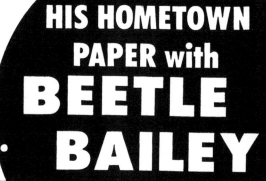

HIS HOMETOWN PAPER with BEETLE BAILEY

Everybody knows discharged Private *by now that the Stars and Stripes (Far East edition)* *Beetle Bailey after a hitch of earnest service . . .*

Now, we are syndicate men, not Military Men —

We don't know why the Sarge;

or maybe the Captain;

or perhaps General Halftrack

busted Beetle, although we could venture a rough guess.

We do know that the GIs miss him. In a news dispatch date lined Tokyo, Sgt. Roland Grief, of Dalles, Ore., said: *"Beetle was one of the first things I looked at when I picked up Stars and Stripes. There are a lot of guys in Korea who are going to miss Beetle. He was good for morale."*

A Major in Korea recently wrote Cartoonist (ex-lieutenant) Mort Walker: *". . . needless to say, your cartoon is the Army's favorite."*

Maj. Gen. H. L. Boatner said: *"it is one of the funniest funnies I have ever seen."*

Newspapers, national magazines and radio commentators have pointed out that Beetle was busted in spite of his high humor ranking. Newsweek, giving the story top play in its press section, wrote: *"some officers, who disliked the decision, said privately that the policy was to ban cartoons that even mildly poked fun at anybody above the Pfc. rank."*

Les Griffith, WABC, New York commented: *"All the GIs know is that Beetle Bailey is missing from their newspaper and they'd like to have him back."*

We know how newspapers across the nation felt about the busting of Beetle. Said the Cleveland Plain Dealer: *"No worthwhile officer objects to a little good-natured kidding . . . We want no army of martinets!"*

Said the Louisville Courier-Journal: *"He {Beetle} is popular with Courier-Journal readers . . . {and} we have heard no cries from on high at Fort Knox. The strip is one of the few left that justifies the old name of 'comics.' Its humor is in the best of temper."*

Said the Daily Spokesman, Pampa, Tex.: *"Enterprising GIs will continue to get copies of Beetle's antics from the news-papers back home until the order is rescinded at some future date."*

There were similar editorials and stories ranging all the way from the New York Journal-American to the Evening News in Manila.

If the boys can't follow Beetle Bailey in Stars and Stripes, why not send that soldier his Hometown Newspaper with Beetle in it? If your newspaper isn't included in the list at left, write or wire F. J. Nicht, General Sales Manager, for terms.

King Features Syndicate 235 EAST 45TH STREET · NEW YORK 17, N. Y.

King Features Syndicate publicity, 1954

Hi and Lois

When the Korean War was over I was sure an army strip would be anathema. I was worried. By now I was used to a few luxuries like eating three times a day. I thought the solution might be to bring Beetle home. and have him become involved in family life.

I created a sister and brother-in-law, Hi and Lois, and their kids, to supply the necessary conflict. After two weeks readers were demanding his return to the Army and I gave in. I still loved doing family gags, though, so I created a new strip and called it "Hi and Lois." The characters have changed a little but it's basically the same.

Dear Folks —

Sorry I haven't written but I've been busy at headquarters on a top level job.

Sarge complimented me on the way I've been doing my work lately

The general got stuck on a big terrain problem Monday. Guess who he called to get him out of the mess!

Killer and I went to Jefferson City last week and saw the Capitol building

You'd like Killer. He's a real thinker. Concentrates for hours!

That's all I can think of to write. Nothing ever happens around here.

Love, Beetle

P.S. Please send me ~~five~~ ten dollars

JULIUS. While Julius is still used in a minor role, he's been fazed out of his original function. I had a fussy roomate once. He was always telling me what to do — open the window — close the window — pick up my clothes — and so on. I started calling him "mother". I thought people might relate to a character like that but they thought he was gay, so now he just drives the general's car.

More Characters Who Bit The Dust

I used to try to create a new character every year, it helped stimulate new interest and gave me fresh material for gags. Most of my gags are built on the interplay and conflict between characters. It began to get confusing with too many characters so I dropped the ones who failed to develop a big following.

BUZZ was replaced by BUNNY

OZONE. I thought it would be funny to introduce a new character as stupid as Zero and have them jointly compound the stupidity. After awhile it seemed only an unnecessary duplication and I dropped Ozone.

MOOCHER. The character that Jack Benny portrayed always amused me so I created a guy named Moocher who was stingy and always borrowing things. Eventually it was hard to think up the gags and I dropped him.

POP. A lot of soldiers are married now and there's a lot of humor in a guy who gets yelled at by Sarge all day and goes home at night for more abuse from his wife. People were so sorry for him they forgot to laugh, and we can't have that.

COSMO. There was a wonderful role created by William Holden in the movie "Stalag 17." He was such a great operator he could get you **ANYTHING**, even in a wartime prison camp. Cosmo was this type until I ran out of ideas.

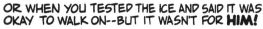

beetle bailey
by mort walker

9-8

beetle bailey® by mort walker

My comic strip is much different today than it was 30 years ago. Back then people had more time and editors gave you more room. I used to draw more big scenes, more detail, and use more dialogue. Today readers devote about 7 seconds to the average strip (we've timed it). If it looks too wordy or complicated they'll skip it. My style now is as crisp and to the point as I can make it. No fooling around with the fun.

beetle bailey
by mort walker

11-9

Otto

Every boy should have a dog, as the saying goes, to teach him love, responsibility and to turn around three times before he lies down. Sarge, being a boy at heart, deserved a dog. But did he deserve Otto? In Otto's puppyhood he was a real dog, walking on all fours and communicating with woofs and growls. It wasn't long before I fell into the old cartoonist's trap and humanized him. I guess he's funnier that way.

Otto first appeared in clothes in the strip above. I was afraid at first to put him in uniform permanently but finally in a 1969 strip (right) I took the chance. The reaction from readers was so tremendous Otto has dressed ever since.

1936 Tip Top Comics Magazine

The Kid Cartoonist

I came from a family of four children and was raised primarily in Kansas City, Missouri. My father was an architect and my mother was a newspaper illustrator when they married. They both painted. My father wrote a great deal and was once appointed "Poet Laureate of Kansas."

Cartoonist Draws Pay As Well as Pictures

It looks like Morton Walker's all set. For two years the 14-year-old has been earning a living with his cartooning.

And a newspaper has a job waiting for him just as soon as he's old enough!

Mort's been drawing ever since he could hold a pencil. But he was 11 before his first cartoon was published.

Since, he's sold more than 70 drawings.

"My first drawings were printed without pay," Mort writes from 3910 Windsor, Kansas City, Mo., "but for the last two years they have brought as much as $5 each.

"Also I have a large collection of rejection slips."

Draws More Than He Plays.

Mort uses his room for a studio, confesses he spends more time drawing than playing. His hobby is collecting cartoon originals by famous artists.

Mort Walker—He Also Gets Rejection Slips.

1938 Syndicated news story

1937 Tip Top Comics Age 14

1936 Kansas City Journal

The old joke goes, "When did you decide to become a cartoonist?" "When I was a baby and was dropped on my head."

There may be more truth than fiction to the joke because I do have a lumpy head and I can't ever remember not being a cartoonist. I was drawing almost before I could talk. It was so natural to me that I was a teenager before I realized that some people weren't cartoonists. I thought it was something that came with the package like ears and feet.

THE LIMEJUICERS.

1937 Kansas City Journal Age 14

The Problem — First Prize

AHHH CHOO
GESUNDHEIT
HAY FEVER !!!

1939 Open Road for Boys Magazine. Monthly contest with prize money. Many now-famous cartoonists entered this contest and became pen pals with each other.

THE THINKERS

All the way through elementary school I drew for the student newspapers, did posters, fliers, anything anyone asked me to do. I sold my first cartoon to a magazine when I was eleven and it ruined me for life. Nobody told me you could make money and have fun at the same time. It's almost illegal, like counterfeiting. I financed all my dates in high school drawing for a dairy magazine and church publications.

1939 Age 16

1940 Cargo Magazine Age 17

Somewhere about that time it occurred to me that drawing was only half the job. A good cartoonist needed to be a good writer as well. I began taking writing courses and studying literature. I became editor of our school newspaper and, later on, editor of my college magazine.

Missin You

VEN YOU HAFF KNOCKED DER MASTER RACE
RIGHT IN DER ZEIDER ZEE,

AND HEILED RIGHT
IN DER FUEHRER'S FACE

PLEASE HURRY
BACK TO ME!

Merry Christmas

My first real art job was with Hallmark Cards. I went to work there when I was eighteen. The writing department was unhappy with the way the art department interpreted their ideas. My job was to sit with the writers and sketch up the cards the way they wanted them. My sketches then went to the art department as guides. Until I left to join the army, almost every card Hallmark produced was based on my design.

Sample of my designs for Hallmark Cards.

A VALENTINE
FOR YOU

WHO'S WHO

$

YOUR FACE IS YOUR FORTUNE
AND YOUR GLORY ---

GOSH, BUT THAT'S
A HARD LUCK
STORY!

1943 Induction Center, Ft. Leavenworth, Kans.

In the Army

Little did I know when I was drafted in 1942 that I was going to get almost four years of free research. I had no idea or ambition at that time to do an army comic strip but I was constantly sketching and trying to capture the humor that was so prevalent in military life. The army thoughtfully sent me to a number of places so that my experiences would be broadest. I was in the Air Corps, Signal Corps, the Engineers, the Infantry, Ordnance, Intelligence and Investigating, and had amphibious training with the Navy. I ended up in charge of a German prisoner of war camp. I was a private, a corporal, a sergeant and a lieutenant and I was a goof-up in every rank.

A.C. TIME

Walker.

When I was in officers' school I illustrated our graduation book with sketches of our four month training period. Naturally, the page satirizing our officer instructors was a favorite with the students. Some of them look prophetically like Beetle Bailey.

Walker

Naples, Italy 1946

Home

ADDISON M.

Overseas

My assignment overseas was with an ordnance depot in Naples, Italy. I was made security officer of the installation in charge of the gates. When the war was over in Europe we began to destroy everything in the depot rather than ship it home or dump it on the Italian market. Binoculars, watches and other small items in our inventory were crushed by driving tanks over them. My job was to see no-one stole anything before it was destroyed. I began to realize that army humor writes itself.

Along with my security duties I was the intelligence and investigating officer. I had rape and murder cases as well as armed raids on the depot by Italian gangsters. The workers in the depot were German prisoners of war and I was in charge of about ten thousand of them. Of course, I wasn't trained for any of these positions, which is typical of army assignments. But at least, at 21 years of age I didn't know what I didn't know, so I muddled through.

Along the way I was picking up ideas for characters.

The German Major Camp Commander

I Base Most of my Characters on Real People

Beetle was patterned after my old high school and army buddy, Dave Hornaday. Dave was tall and skinny and was always getting into trouble innocently.

Sgt. Snorkel was inspired by a top sergeant I once had, Sgt. Octavian Savou. He was tough as nails but thought of us as "his boys."

When I wanted a young neophyte lieutenant I thought back on all the dumb things I did as a 20-year-old shavetail, and created Lt. Fuzz.

My partner Dik Browne sneaked into the strip via the brainy Plato.

Chaplain Staneglass came out of Barry Fitzgerald's performance as a priest in "Going My Way."

Marilyn Monroe was the godmother to Miss Buxley.

Jesse Wrench was an eccentric Professor at M.U.

College Days

After my army stint I enrolled in the Journalism school at the University of Missouri, one of the finest in the world. I lasted about a month until they discovered I didn't have the proper prerequisites (instead of studying I'd been off funning around in the army) and they kicked me out. Even so, I retained my membership in Sigma Delta Chi, the honorary journalism fraternity and my position as editor-in-chief of the school magazine, THE SHOW-ME. After graduation I went to New York and got a job with Dell Publishing Co. as editor of several fan and humor magazines. On the side I sold cartoons to the top magazines. Many of my cartoons contained scenes of the M.U. campus and many of my characters were patterned after teachers and school friends. Two years later I was vindicated when I was invited to be a guest speaker at Missouri Journalism Week and they later gave me an award as an honored graduate.

My Office in Journalism Building

FATHER'S DAY

"ONE DAY EACH YEAR THE FAMILY SHOWERS ME ___ WITH SO MANY FAVORS _____ PRESENTS _____ AND SIGNS OF AFFECTION___

___THAT SOMETIMES IT TAKES ME ____NEARLY A WEEK _____ TO REGAIN MY NORMAL _____ COMPOSURE!"

THE SATURDAY
EVENING POST

Getting Going

My cartooning career in New York began in 1948 with magazine cartoons. Each Wednesday the editors would hold open house for cartoonists. Anyone with a batch of cartoons could see an editor without appointment. I would start early in the morning at the Saturday Evening Post, the big magazine at the time, and saw around 20 editors during the day. It took about three months before I was selling regularly, but one year I sold more than anyone else in the business.

The first strip I submitted for syndication about a teen-age boy was turned down because the syndicate already had a teen-age strip.

"Okay, Spider, heads we join the Army,
tails we go on studying for final exams."

THE SATURDAY EVENING POST

MORT WALKER

John Bailey, the SEP editor, remembered my work in college and suggested I draw some cartoons in that setting. He bought a few and spotted one character with his hat over his eyes. "Funny guy. Why don't you feature him." he said. I did, and called him "Spider" after a fraternity brother.

One day a lightbulb turned on over my head. "Why not do a comic strip about college and put all my fraternity brothers in it?" King Features bought it, and changed Spider's name to Beetle. I added the Bailey in honor of John Bailey.

BEETLE BAILEY   FRESHMAN   DIAMOND JIM   BITTER BILL

BEETLE BAILEY   **They're the Considerate Type!**   By Mort Walker

SHHH, PLATO IS STUDYING.

LET'S NOT BOTHER HIM!

LET'S JUST SIT HERE AND HAVE A NICE QUIET BULL SESSION.

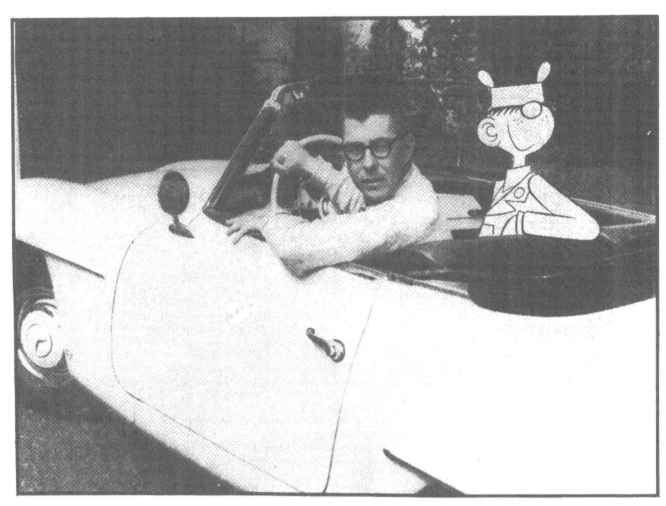

Photograph from a 1960 newspaper story

The Life of a Cartoonist

I was ecstatic to have my own comic strip and be able to work at home. No more commuting to my magazine job in New York City. The awful crush of the subways, waiting for buses in the rain, the waste of time were other people's problems now.

But soon I discovered a new set of problems. I was completely on my own. I could sink or swim depending on my own ability to paddle. It's tough to discipline yourself to get up in the morning, get to work rather than read newspapers till noon, and stay at work resisting the many temptations for fun. It's tough to discipline the family, too. Daddy's available for play, baby sitting, shopping, conversation. Even neighbors get in on the act when they see male-power around to help carry things, fix cars or draw posters. If you're not in New York you can't be WORKING.

I decided regular office hours of 9 to 5 was something everyone, including myself, would accept. The trouble with working for yourself, though, is you're never through working. Sometimes you work 24 hours a day, weekends, and holidays. Sometimes you sit staring out the window waiting all day for an idea to come.

The best part is being able to see your kids grow up. Jean and I had seven. Many men are gone so much they become strangers to their families. I think I can remember the names of each of my children.

Success brings pressures, too. There's no doubt that having money is better, but it still creates problems with family and friends, jealousies, demands on you. It's difficult not to spoil your children. You want so badly to give them everything but it destroys their incentive and robs them of the pride of getting things on their own.

We decided we wanted a family life rather than high society and we wanted to keep our old friends. We didn't change our way of life much for over 30 years.

The Comics Business

Editors are a necessary evil, I suppose. Too often they prevent you from printing your best stuff under the pretense that it's too dirty. They always ruin your most creative spelling attempts by pulling a dictionary on you. And they can read your most hilarious, side-splitting gags and keep that wonderful corpse-like expression that all editors have. I suppose it's better having editors than having those people out in the streets scaring dogs but I still wouldn't want my sister marrying one.

The best editing is done by the public. They let you know immediately if you've done something wrong or right. After all, they're the ones you want to please, anyway, not the editor. There's no way you can please an editor. He's too busy looking for missing commas and anti-acid plus to enjoy anything. They all hate cartoonists, anyway.

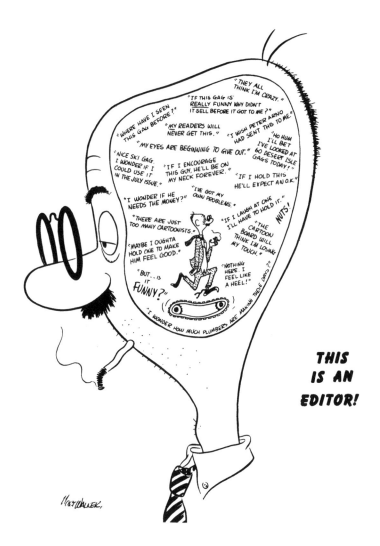

THIS IS AN EDITOR!

Harry Hershfield, the cartoonist and raconteur, told me he had a very popular strip in a New York paper back in the days when no-one was allowed to sign stories or editorials. The editor decided it was time his newspapermen deserved some credit so he decreed they could all have bylines.

Harry asked if that meant HE could have a byline. The editor said "No, only newspapermen." Harry asked, "But my cartoon appears in your paper. Doesn't that make me a newspaperman?"

The editor sneered, "is a barnacle a SHIP?"

As editors see us.

As we see ourselves . . .

EDITOR & PUBLISHER for March 9, 1963

Comics have changed over the years. Story strips and joke strips aren't as popular as they once were. The trend today is to mirror a segment of life that editors want to reach, like the unmarried working girl. Many creators are using the autobiographic approach, writing humor with deeply personal meaning. A lot of the creations therefore, have a striking resemblance to the creators. I wish God had thought of that.

SAM'S STRIP was a comic strip about comic strips Jerry Dumas and I produced from 1961 to 1963.

The comic strip business is unique. No-one knows what will make a good strip. If you SAY you know, sure enough next week someone will create a winner that blasts all your theories to hell. I never thought "Peanuts" would be the success it is. I couldn't believe "Doonesbury" when I first saw it. Now they're two of my favorite strips.

Strips like that succeed, I think, because the highly fascinating personality of the creator is allowed to come through. I don't think a dull person could do a good comic strip.

Some comic strip artists won't allow themselves exposure like that. They get locked into a format and turn out their strip like sausages on an assembly line. I like to feel like that 2 x7 inch space is mine to do whatever I like. When I sit at the board I rule a universe. Everybody does what I want them to. I can take the human figure and stretch it out of shape, have it blown up and reassembled in the next panel if I want. It's an awesome power much like God has when he sits at that great drawing board in the sky and gives life to all us wretches.

The King Features East Staff

from left to right:

Bud Jones: Writes for Beetle, Hi and Lois, and Boner's Ark

Mort Walker: Draws Beetle, writes gags for Beetle, and Hi and Lois. Supervises Boner's Ark and The Evermores. Writes and draws the Beetle albums.

Bob Gustafson: Writes gags for Beetle, Hi and Lois, and Boner's Ark. Writes and draws Beetle comic book. Answers fan mail and does special drawing assignments.

Jerry Dumas: Writes gags for Beetle, Hi and Lois and Boner's Ark. Writes and draws Sam and Silo.

Greg Walker: Writes gags for Beetle, and Hi and Lois. Inks Beetle Sunday page. Letters Beetle and does special drawing assignments.

Frank Johnson: Inks Beetle and Hi and Lois. Draws and inks Boner's Ark. Inks Beetle comic books and albums.

King Features Syndicate publicity, 1956

A cartoonist once told me to work very hard for the first year or so till you get your strip off the ground, then you can relax, hire someone to do it for you, and have a life of ease. That cartoonist soon lost his strip and never got another one.

My experience is, the more successful you get, the harder you have to work. As I zoomed past the 500 paper mark I began to feel a tremendous responsibility to my readers, almost a stage fright. If I've done this good today I've got to do at least as good tomorrow, or better, if I can. If you're not moving forward in this business, you are moving backwards.

4-9

King Features Syndicate publicity, 1957

Success is fun but it can be very heady. A cartoonist can't succomb to the feeling of importance or he will destroy his most valuable asset. Our job is to knock down idols, and punch holes in pomposity. If we begin to believe our own publicity we go over to the enemy. I think every one of the cartoonists who write humorous comics are very warm, humble human beings.

Has Beetle been discharged?

Home on Furlough

Once in a while I take Beetle home on furlough for Christmas, and usually Sarge goes with him. It's the only time I've ever done a "story" or sequential strips. It's more work than gag-a-day because every day has to move the story ahead, yet still be funny. Some readers are disappointed. They only want a laugh a day. Others remember these sequences for years .. what to do?

Is Sgt. Orville Snorkel A.W.O.L?

1964 Furlough

1965 Furlough

King Features Syndicate publicity, 1959

Many people wonder why a military strip like Beetle appeals to a civilian audience. The truth is, it isn't a military strip. It's a strip about a bunch of funny guys. They could be policemen, factory workers, college students, whatever. The army is just a convenient setting that everyone understands. The pecking order doesn't have to be explained and the role of the poor guy at the bottom of the ladder is classic in literature.

3-15

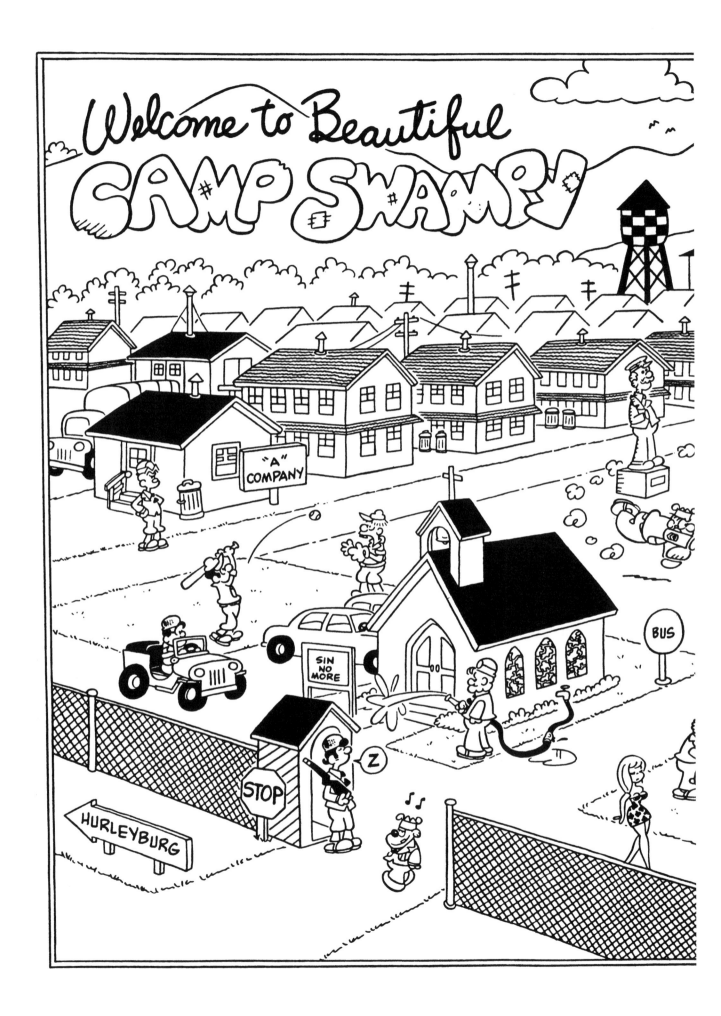

7-29

King Features Syndicate publicity, 1963

The army never officially endorsed Beetle Bailey in spite of its rising popularity. The closest I ever came to acceptance was the Pentagon circulating a few of my strips to show how NOT to do things. A Pentagon representative once approached King Features and urged them to produce a strip with a heroic infantryman as the star. In a way I'm happy I never became a spokesman for the military. It would have killed the humor.

7-5

1000 Editors say He's Tops!

Until Beetle crossed the grand line in the 60's, only one feature in comic strip history, "Blondie", had ever appeared in a thousand newspapers. Now there were two. Soon "Peanuts" joined the select group. Many years later we welcomed "Hagar the Horrible," "Garfield," and "Hi and Lois."

A strip reaches the "saturation point" around 1,600 papers. There just isn't anyplace left to sell them.

King Features Syndicate publicity, 1965

King Features Syndicate publicity, 1968

Beetle Bailey has been studied by sociologists for the way authority is represented. Americans feel that authority should be questioned, not blindly followed, and people in authority in this country, accept this resistance as an inalienable right. In Europe and many Asian countries, the class system and regal sovereignty are so deeply ingrained, many citizens never question an order. In Italy there is a soldier comic strip where the private always ends up in jail for things that Beetle does routinely. Beetle and Sarge play the game, Sarge doing his job imposing authority and Beetle doing his, resisting it.

1-10

SARGE WENT INTO TOWN, BEETLE

WHY DIDN'T HE SAY SO IN THE FIRST PLACE?

PX

12-3

A little satire can be fun occasionally. I used the head of MAD Magazine symbol, Alfred E. Newman, in my strip once. It brought in mountains of mail. Then MAD magazine invited me to create a new strip for them and I did the version below of "The Heart of Juliet Jones." Stan Drake, my golfing buddy and creator of Juliet, retaliated with this page in "The Cartoonist magazine.

MORT WALKER—creator of

"BEETLE BAILEY"

"I've always wanted to do a "Heart of Juliet Jones"-type strip called "The Chapped Hands of Sybil Sudsy." I guess working with an all-male cast for 14 years finally got to me. But this project was a good thing for me because it made me realize how lucky I am doing a strip for a living where it's not necessary to know how to draw!"

© King Features Syndicate, Inc. 1966. World rights reserved.

THEY ARE **SITTING DUCKS!**

3-27

beetle bailey
by MORT WALKER

Now in
1337
Newspapers
And
Still Climbing!

To Sarge, Beetle may be just a shiftless, incompetent goof-off, but in polls conducted by many newspapers throughout the world, millions of readers have voted Beetle Bailey their favorite comic strip character.

Another Success Story From KING

What makes a successful comic strip? Rube Goldberg said once, "Don't try to analyze it, it's pure magic."

We all know the ingredients. You must create interesting characters that readers care about. The gags should be rewarding enough to make the reader feel he hasn't wasted his time. The drawing doesn't have to be great but it should put across the idea.

It sounds simple but only a handful of cartoonists have done it. Out of about 2,000 submissions each year, syndicates launch about 30 strips. Of those, about one in every five years becomes really successful.

As of this printing (1983) Beetle Bailey appeared in 1637 newspapers.

THE HOME STRETCH

The Eternal Beetle

Will Beetle ever get promoted? Will he ever get married? Become a civilian again? These are questions often asked. Sometimes I get petitions from groups of soldiers requesting he be promoted. Beetle will never do any of these things. In a world that's changing too fast it's good to have something permanent. Beetle and the rock of Gibralter will remain immobile throughout eternity.

The Loveable Sarge

Who could love an overweight old sergeant with a snaggle tooth and the manners of a hippopotamus? Nobody, unless pity and disgust add up to love. The closest Sarge will ever get to love is a late-night rehash of Killer's exploits.

2-1

Dear Sarge!
    I have stoodfor just about as muchas i can! what happent todayi just cannotbe fogottin or forgivven.

You seem toenjoy bawlinng out guys for the funnn of it! well, i for one have hade just about enoughj!

The next time youu see meyoubegger duck becuase i plan to come ouut swinging& i'mm givingh you fare warniiing/?

you# are5 problayt goinjg tobe serprizxxed   to gety hnmj frommebecjhawu@ you thuojkt i wasonypi7uwjsice,well, you got anothurew thinkcominj" SO wartchouy stepk/???

AS ever,
Beetle

5-24

The Ultimate Otto

When I first sketched Sarge's dog, I took one look and thought, "He looks like Otto Soglow!" Soglow was a famous New Yorker cartoonist and creator of the comic strip, "The Little King." He wasn't very tall, less than five feet, and he wasn't very handsome, but everybody loved Otto. He was brutally honest, hilariously cantankerous and often incoherent. He also may be the only human being who was the inspiration for a comic strip dog.

WELL, GOODNIGHT, GIRLS

SMAK

3-5

DON'T I GET A KISS?

SORRY. I GAVE AT THE OFFICE

TO THINK, ONE OF THE REASONS I MARRIED HER WAS HER SENSE OF HUMOR

© King Features Syndicate, Inc., 1975. World rights reserved.

The Matronly Martha

Recently I read that someone had called Nancy Reagan on the phone and heard her say, "Ronnie, will you turn down your TV, I'm on the phone." While this is a mild example, it illustrates the humorous situation I'm trying to portray. Many men of power and prestige are reduced to peonage the minute they open the door of their home. The General may command thousands of men and be supreme over Camp Swampy but at home Martha is definitely in charge.

TUNNEL OF LOVE

50¢

WHAT DO YOU SAY, MARTHA?

NOT TONIGHT. I HAVE A HEADACHE

10-31   © King Features Syndicate, Inc., 1975. World rights reserved.

MORT WALKER

THE CAPTAIN SAID YOU'RE HAVING TROUBLE WITH YOUR DISHWASHER

YES

5-28

I THINK I KNOW WHAT THE PROBLEM IS, GENERAL

YOUR WIFE'S AWAY

MORT WALKER

© 1979 King Features Syndicate, Inc. World rights reserved.

The Venerable General

They say that most of the great characters in literature are autobiographical. Gen. Halftrack is my attempt to reach those heights. He is me. He loves his golf, he loves his martinis and he loves to look at pretty girls even though he knows he's over the hill. I sympathize with the old coot although I know sympathy isn't exactly what he wants.

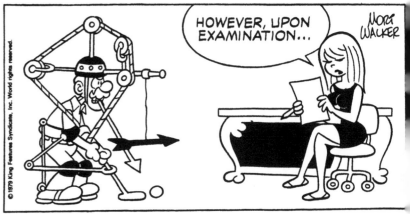

by mort walker

Miss Buxley

The latest broughaha has been over Miss Buxley. I first introduced her in 1971 with no idea of making her a regular character. Readers liked her, though, so I began using her more and more until she showed up once a week. Suddenly in 1982 letters began pouring in from feminists saying that she was a sexual sterotype and that I was promoting sexual harassment. They forced a few editors to censor the strip which caused an even bigger furor. Polls were taken in five papers and readers responded with an overwhelming 85% approval of Miss Buxley. Magazines and newspapers ran articles about her and there were numerous radio and TV interviews. (It all resulted in a book, "Miss Buxley: Sexism in Beetle Bailey?".) I'm just trying to write a funny comic strip and if people are going to act that way, I have to draw about it.

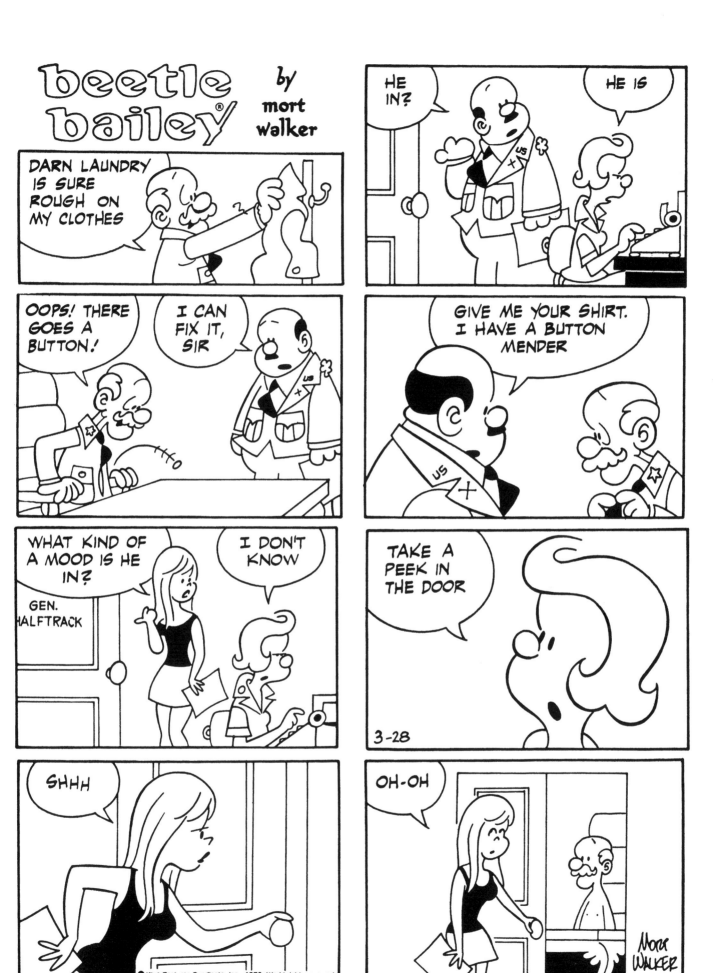

The New Army

I don't try to keep up with the new systems or weapons in the army, preferring to base my humor on people, who never change. Still it's fun to note the Pentagon's attempts to become more efficient because, when THEY make a mistake, it's monumental!

Dr. Bonkus

Every camp has a psychiatrist and no camp needs one more than Camp Swampy. Of course they got the psychiatrist they deserve, Dr. Bonkus, who could use a little help himself.

First Appearance

Lt. Flap

Many people had urged me for years to put a black in my strip. The trouble was, if I made him a lazy goof-off like the regular cast I'd get complaints. Finally I thought of creating a macho type who liked wild clothes and Lt. Flap was born. There was an initial fuss from people who either thought I was propogandizing or ridiculing blacks. The STARS AND STRIPES banned me again and Senator Proxmire had to convince them to re-instate me. Now the flurry has died down and Lt. Flap is a favorite with many.

The Diet

It seems like everyone in America is on a diet these days and Sarge reflects their hopes and failures. I allowed him to lose weight once and got a petition from a weight watchers group with 400 signatures pleading with me to let him succeed. Of course I couldn't comply. Sarge without his poundage just wasn't Sarge — nor was he as funny — so back went the fat where it belonged.

Visual Humor

An editor told me a long time ago that, if you could cover up the drawing and still get the gag by reading the caption, then you were a writer and not a cartoonist. With that advice I've always tried to get as many funny pictures in my work as possible. To me, the best gag is one you laugh at immediately and chuckle at later.

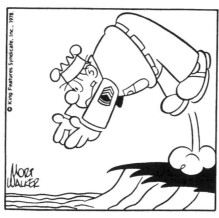

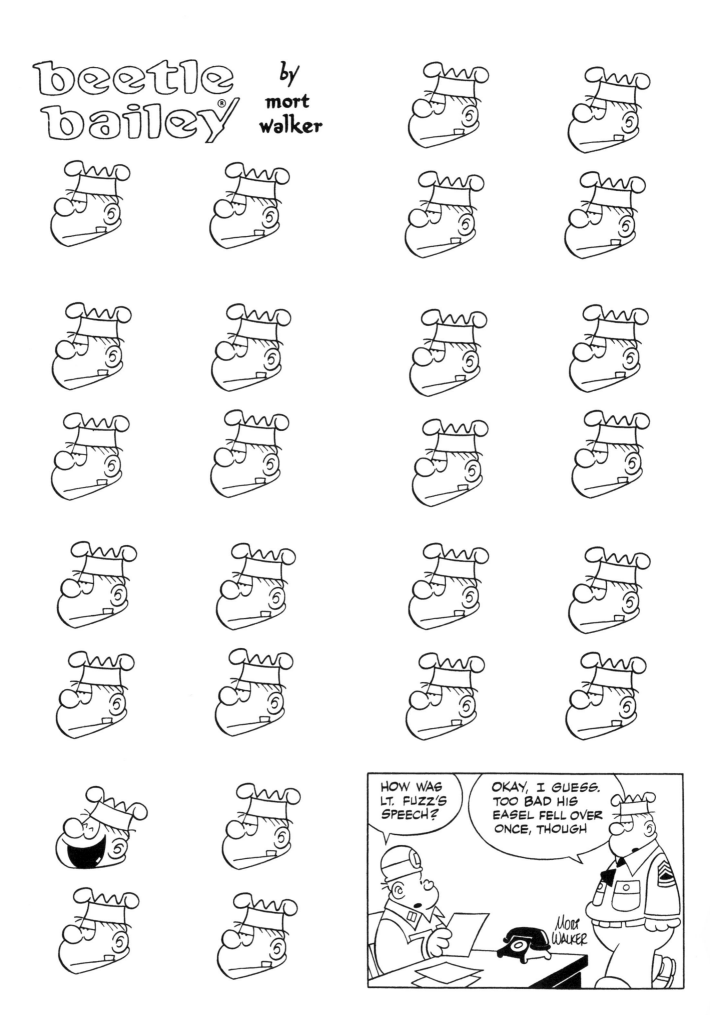

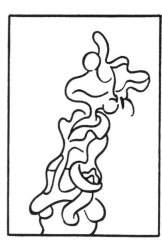

New Freedoms, Old Taboos

When I got into this business the taboos were awesome. You couldn't draw snakes, skunks, dirty socks, alcohol, nudity, divorce, cleavage, toilets, etc., etc. My big contribution to progress was the navel. Whenever I put one on a girl in a bathing suit the editors would cut if off the drawing with a razor blade. One day I visited our syndicate office and saw a box on the editor's desk labeled "Beetle Bailey's Belly Button Box." In it were piles of little black dots — the offensive navels! Since the editor seemed to enjoy this exercise I began giving my girls several navels and more spare ones in the margin. One day I drew Cookie receiving a big shipment of navel oranges, navels all over the place. The editor gave up the battle. Now I can draw my girls with everything they were born with.

Comics are still our cleanest form of literature. Editors believe that comics are for kids, which they're not. A few cartoonists, like Garry Trudeau, have cut a path into the present but the rest of us are limping along carrying our load of Victorian taboos making just enough progress to keep us out of the dark age.

Philosophy in the Comics
    Al Capp once said, "You can't draw a picture of a dog without making a statement on the condition of dogs." All cartoons therefore contain observations on mankind and society. Some cartoons are just more obvious in this regard.

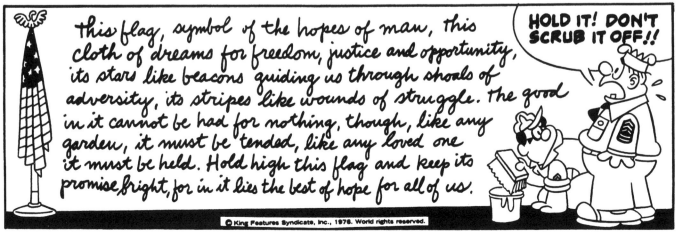

by mort walker

Friendship

Friendship is a footbridge joining isolated bodies together allowing free and confident passage, sharing what each has, and adding to the sum total of each.

To be a friend one must be as tolerant to the other as to himself. thus the self is made larger and stronger. A good friend is one who will lend as though giving and repay more than is lent!

Cherish your friends... they make up a man's wealth more surely than gold...for a man without a friend is like a cork without a bottle.

© King Features Syndicate, Inc., 1977.

It is not necessary to tell a friend you like him. He knows. But tell him anyway. Friendship, like plants, blooms greater when nourished.

11-13

Defend your friends, elevate your friends, help your friends, and you will find even your enemies will want to be your friends.

I JUST WANTED YOU TO PAINT "FRIENDSHIP" ON THE SIDE OF MY VAN!

WELL...ONCE I GOT STARTED...

MORT WALKER

Social Comment

Beetle Bailey, by its very nature, is a commentary on the military establishment in this country, a playful satire on bureaucracy and the system. I also throw in some other pithy comments on race, war, sex and various social problems without getting too heavy handed. I want my strip to be fun, not preachy.

Cartoon Violence

People are understandably concerned about the violence children and society are exposed to. Certain people may absorb or imitate things they see or read. Others may enjoy a catharsis of pent-up emotions. It's an interesting debate. The last thing I want to do is contribute to our already over-violent world. But I refuse to believe that cartoon violence will lead anyone to similar behavior any more than Bugs Bunny makes people eat carrots.

Cartoon Art

It's fun occasionally to take pot-shots at our own profession. Al Capp satirized "Dick Tracy" with his "Fearless Fosdick" sequences. Chester Gould made fun of "Peanuts" with episodes of "Sawdust." Snoopy goes off on Veteran's Day to have a root beer with Bill Mauldin. Many cartoonists have cameo guest appearances of other comic characters. It may confuse a few readers for a day or so but the readers who "get" the gag are doubly pleased.

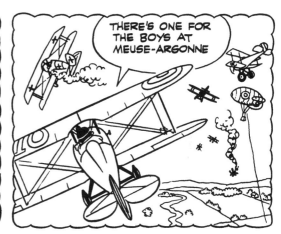

The Characters Collide

There are a lot of characters in Beetle, more than any other strip. But who ever heard of an army without people? Naturally they come in conflict with one another which makes for a lot of funny happenings.

THIS WAS THE FOURTH OR SIXTH TIME I DARNED THOSE SOCKS. THERE'S HARDLY ANY SOCKS LEFT. I'M WALKING AROUND ON **DARNS!** HA-HA, YEAH, THAT WAS A GOOD ONE. YEAH, I'LL REMEMBER IT. I'LL TELL SARGE, **DARN SHAME.** HE'LL LIKE THAT... HE'S OUT TODAY, BUT I'LL WAIT UP AND TELL HIM WHEN HE GETS IN

I WAS DARNING SOCKS BECAUSE IT WAS RAINING. NOTHING ELSE TO DO. DID YOU EVER DARN SOCKS WHEN YOU WERE YOUNG? YOU DID? WAS IT RAINING? IT **WAS**? WELL, I'LL BE DARNED! **HOLY MACKEREL,** THERE'S ANOTHER ONE! HA HA HA HA! I'M FULL OF THEM, HUH? YOU SAY I TAKE AFTER **YOU?** YOU CAN SAY THAT AGAIN! YES, SIR, YOU CAN SAY THAT AGAIN!

HEY, NOW **YOU'RE** SAYING IT AGAIN! BOY, ARE WE EVER A PAIR, HUH, DAD? TELL MOM WHAT WE'VE BEEN TALKING ABOUT. NO, I'LL WRITE HER ALL ABOUT IT SO SHE'LL HAVE A PERMANENT COPY. OKAY, I MISS YOU, TOO. YOU GOING OUT TO FEED THE HOGS NOW? SOCK IT TO 'EM! HA HA! SO LONG.

Do We Need To Show The Banana?
by Jerry Dumas

Left to right: Bob Gustafson, Greg Walker, Mort Walker, Bud Jones, Jerry Dumas.

Larry Gelbart, the brilliant original writer of TV's M*A*S*H, quit writing that show after 97 episodes, saying that he was tired out and leery of repeating himself.

Garry Trudeau, creator of Doonesbury, has after 12 years put that strip on hold, saying that at age 34, it's a young man's game.

Other steady producers of humor can understand and sympathize. It is an exhausting business. When Russell Baker goes on vacation there are guest columnists. When Art Buchwald departs for Martha's Vineyard each summer he leaves behind a judicious selection of favorite old columns. That's okay — it's fun to see them again.

But with pardonable pride, Mort Walker has managed a fresh Beetle Bailey strip every single day for 33 years. That's seven days a week, no duplication, no repeats. And no small accomplishment.

That's just for Beetle Bailey. Gag ideas have also been generated for the 29 years of Hi and Lois' existence, and for 15 years of Boner's Ark. That means that for the last 15 years, ideas have been used up at the rate of 21 a week.

Where do the ideas come from? That is probably the single most frequently-asked question a cartoonist hears. In Beetle's case, here's the low-down on where they come from and how they are selected:

Mort Walker created Beetle Bailey in 1950. Fred Rhoads helped him briefly, then Frank Roberge for a year and a half helped with the drawing and wrote gags. In July of 1956, fresh out of Arizona State College, I washed up on Mort's studio steps, a survivor of four years of English courses but with no published cartoons worth mentioning.

I had been a fan of Mort's since the moment I first saw a cartoon of his in the Saturday Evening Post. I was sitting at the counter of a drug store in Detroit, wearing a long white apron and drinking a Boston Cooler (Vernor's ginger ale, one scoop of chocolate). I was on my coffee break from the Kroger's grocery next door, and they used to let me read the magazines. I turned a page and saw the work of a new cartoonist. He signed his name simply 'Mort'. I remember muttering, "This guy is good." I ran my eye along each line in the cartoon, mentally re-drawing it. At that moment he began being a big influence in my life.

Through the fifties and into the sixties Mort and I would each write 10 gags a week. We needed 14 for Beetle and for Hi and Lois, so we could reject or save 6. Life seemed simple.

Then it got a little complicated. And quite a bit more fun.

For a year and a half, we also wrote and drew Sam's Strip. Then Bob Gustafson, who had been writing funny gags for Tillie the Toiler, and drawing it too, came aboard. In 1967, with Boner's Ark about to be launched, witty Bud Jones was added to the crew. From then on, the four of us wrote and sketched out 70 gags a week, stockpiling the best ones through the winter months so that we could let up some in the summer. Greg Walker, Mort's eldest son, also writes gags for all the strips, demonstrating the fine Walker comic touch.

So these are the people involved; now, how do the gags get into the people?

Basically, we're in the truth business. We do get downright silly sometimes, but what we're really up to is this: here is how a lazy man thinks; here is how a pompus lieutenant acts; how dumb can army regulations be? Here's how dumb; if a typical husband does *this,* a typical wife might respond like *that.*

So we each sit in our homes, studying blank sheets of paper. We keep trying to think of a combination of words and pictures nobody has ever done before. We try to think of a ridiculous, preposterous picture, an absurd situation, something that would be the direct result of a character's previous action. But the first two panels must be believable. If it sounds and looks contrived, the reader will not believe the conclusion, and the gag will be second-rate. If nothing else is working at the moment, we just get any two characters talking to each other. It's surprising to see where conversations will go, given personalities to work with like Sarge and Zero and General Halftrack.

So we draw up the gags, get initial reactions from members of the family, and head for the Monday morning gag conference.

We all think that this is a highlight of the week. It is pleasant to have visible proof that your week's work has been accomplished. There is always a note of expectancy in the air: perhaps this week one of us has come up with not just a funny gag, but a true gem. That rarely happens, but we keep watching and waiting and hoping.

We grade each other's ideas. Each gets a 1+, a 1, a 1-, or a 2. That's it. No other grades. A 2 is the kiss of death. It's out, unless someone can think of a way to improve it. One hopes that it won't be a personal favorite. We all of us are frank, blunt and kind. It turns out that it is possible to be all three.

A gag idea with all 1's or all 2's on it presents no problem. But we now arrive at a gag with a variety of opinions attached to it.

"There's something there."

"I didn't get it."

"Didn't you see the banana?"

"Is that a banana? It didn't look like a banana."

"It's a half-eaten banana."

"To show someone eating a banana, don't you have to show the skin hanging down over his hand? Where's the skin?"

"When I eat a banana, I take the skin all off. I throw it away. This skin was thrown away already."

"I don't think the reader is going to know that's a banana. And he *has* to. Maybe you could indicate those little lines a banana has."

"Banana skins have lines. Bananas don't."

"Sure they do. Those little soft stringy things you strip off."

"Do we actually need to *show* the banana? Banana is already said in the first panel."

"Listen, we could change it to an egg."

One can see why we do not dare hold business lunches in restaurants. We tried it once: stockbrokers and insurance executives kept changing tables.

That is pretty much how it goes. We try to tell the truth, we try to be a bit silly, we try to be irreverent, we try to point out naked emperors. Mark Twain had something to say about it all:

"The American press has laughed a thousand cruel and infamous shams into the grave. Irreverence is the champion of liberty and its only sure defense."

It's a fine thing to be — a cartoonist in a free country. If a Russian Mort Walker had created a Russian Beetle Bailey, throwing barbs at the Red Army and the Kremlin for the last 33 years — and getting *away* with it — oh, what a lovely world climate it would be.

MISSION ACCOMPLISHED

30 Years and Holding

While much has changed in the 30 plus years Beetle has been going, it's surprising how many things have remained the same. The General still hasn't heard from the Pentagon, Sarge hasn't had a date, Beetle hasn't washed his socks, Cookie still cooks bouncy meatballs . . . some themes will never die.

Contemporary Twists

I try to keep abreast of current topics and mores so I won't become old-fashioned. Occasionally I overstep the boundaries, as I did in the strip below. Several editors refused to print it this way. I substituted "leg of lamb" in Cookie's balloon in the last panel and they accepted that, although it wasn't nearly as funny.

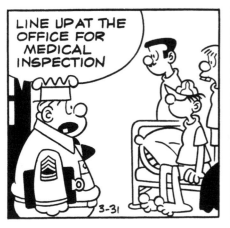

Censored Gags

Occasionally we get an idea that shouldn't be printed in a family newspaper. We thought you might like to see a few that had to be rejected.

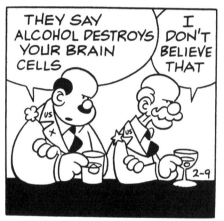

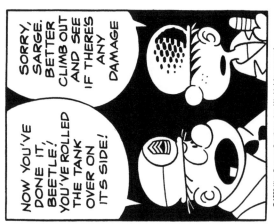

New Challenges

While I must adhere to a certain format, I like to think of my strip area as my space to do what I want and to have fun both visually and verbally. I feel if I have fun with my strip my readers probably will too. I never want to get locked in or bored with my work and I never have. After 33 years I still rush eagerly to the studio every morning to create new havoc for Beetle and Sarge . . . and I hope it lasts for another 33 years.

New Characters

Every year or so it's fun to bring in new blood. It keeps the strip fresh and gives me new opportunities for humor. The latest arrival is Rolf, the tennis pro, my answer to the feminists who claim I'm a sexist in my treatment of Miss Buxley. Okay, tit for tat is fair. Rolf is a hunk who is treated as a sex object. So far no complaints. I guess men don't mind being sex objects.

The Final Bulletin

Flash . . . Beetle Bailey cartoon novels done for Europe soon to be launched in U.S. . . . CBS Prime Time special in the works . . . Broadway show in the wings . . . Beetle's "Complete Guide to Loafing" due out . . . Arcade game proposed . . . Dolls, toys, and other products contracted for . . . one-man show of Beetle originals scheduled for New York Gallery . . . . . . stay tuned for further developments . . .

The Road Ahead

This whole book has been devoted to looking backward and it seems only fair that we give the future a few words. What lies ahead for Beetle besides more naps and knocks?

For one thing, I hope comics will still be around five years from now. With the rapid way things are moving in the electronics field we may get all our news from a tv set very soon. Who knows what that will do to comic strips. Maybe we'll have a tv version of dial-a-joke with people punching a button to get their daily Beetle Bailey fix.

However, I predict we will always have some sort of newspaper put in our hands and it will probably contain comics. You can't wrap a fish in a tv set and you can't swat a fly with a computer. We need newspapers.

So I think we can look forward to another 30 years of military mischief. Some new characters will arrive as others depart. We'll make fun of the government, new fashions, food, sex, and anything that deserves to be ridiculed.

As our thinking becomes more liberal we will be doing gags on subjects that were once taboo. Maybe someday I'll show Killer "making out" with a girl as many soldiers do in real life. Maybe Sarge will use actual swear words instead of symbols. Maybe men libbers will get after me for stereotyping lazy GI's.

All I know is, it won't be dull.
Stick around.

Mort Walker
Jan. 1, 1984

I WANT THAT STAR TO SHINE BEETLE!
BLOW IT OUT YOUR ATOMIC REACTOR!
2025
MORT WALKER

THE MUSEUM OF CARTOON ART

In August 1974, after a decade of planning and fund-raising, spearheaded by the Museum's President and resident cartoonist, Mort Walker, the world's first Museum dedicated solely to the unique art form of cartooning was opened to the public. Since that time, the Museum of Cartoon Art has gained an international reputation as the finest center for the collection, exhibition and preservation of all forms of cartoon art.

The Museum features exhibits of original artwork from all of the various genres of cartoon art, including comic strips, comic books, animation, caricature, illustration and more. In addition to exhibits and film and video programs, a library is open to researchers by appointment. The gift shop and original art sales gallery is open to the public during operating hours.

Located in the historic "Ward's Castle" on Comly Avenue in Rye Brook, N.Y., the Museum is open from Tuesday to Friday, 10 AM to 4 PM and Sundays 1 PM to 5 PM. Admission is $1.50 for adults and 75¢ for children and senior citizens. For more information call (914) 939-0234.

978-0-595-34848-0
0-595-34848-3

Made in the USA
Lexington, KY
05 November 2012